Think YOU could survive the monster apocalypse?

Can you invent zombie-fighting gadgets like Quint?

Design a tricked-out "end of the world" vehicle like Dirk?

Craft the perfect post-apocalyptic playlist like June?

Come up with heroic one-liners like Jack?

Hint: You can do it all (and more!) with the help of this handy-dandy guide complete with creative challenges, do-it-yourself activities, and tons of cool facts about your favorite characters and monsters! So, what are you waiting for?

IT'S GO TIME!

Logan Collins

MAX BRALLIER

& DOUGLAS HOLGATE

present:

Let's do this thing.

VIKING

VIKING
An imprint of Penguin Random House LLC, New York

First published in the United States of America by Viking,
an imprint of Penguin Random House LLC, 2019

Visit us online at penguinrandomhouse.com

ISBN 9781984835406

Printed in the USA

10   9   8   7   6   5   4   3   2   1

Book design by Jim Hoover

To Alyse, the best.

THIS BOOK BELONGS TO:

Logan
_____

A great book always seems to get messed up . . . Y'know—the book gets mashed in your backpack or Dirk sits on it or Rover slobbers on it or you get pizza grease on the pages.

Well, this is a GREAT BOOK—so let's mess it up RIGHT NOW!

Drool on this page and try to hit the bullseye—for real!

Drool here.

Good! This book's "mess up" is out of the way. Onward—time to do this thing!

MEET THE HEROES!

JACK! JUNE! QUINT! DIRK!
WITTY BANTER! GOOD TIMES!

JACK SULLIVAN

JUNE DEL TORO

Brain is smart. Total smart brain.

Louisville Slicer™, the greatest monster-fighting weapon in all the land!

Hockey stick, for conking zombie heads.

Walkie-talkie. Direct line to best friend Quint.

Emergency Peanut M&M pouch.

Worst. Shoes. Ever.

Monster head—but I didn't slice this one off. I just found it like that!

Boys' sneakers. She is rad like that.

 FUN FACT: The original title for the series was The Tree House at the End of the World.

4

5

NOW YOU'RE THE HERO!

What if *you* were one of the last kids on earth? Draw yourself. Or tape in a selfie. Add your own arrows and labels!

NEED SOME INSPIRATION, FRIEND? Here are a few ideas!

• Harpoon with zip line. For escaping UP!
• Air-conditioned underwear. For cool comfort in the heat of battle.
• Rearview mirror. No more being snuck up on by giant monsters or annoying siblings.

Cut this page out and hang it on your door!

BEST BUDDY QUIZ!

How close are you and your best friend, really? Take this quiz and find out! Circle one answer (A, B, C, or D) per question.

1. Your best friend has a tick stuck to his/her rear end. Do you remove it?

Ⓐ Yep. Will use a Quint-Inspired Automatic Distant Turbo-Charged Tick Remover.

Ⓑ Yes. Of course! (I think.)

Ⓒ No. Not even in the dark while wearing gloves.

Ⓓ Nope. Time for a new best friend.

2. Your buddy's breath stinks like hot garbage! What do you do?

(A) Have a heart-to-heart talk. ('Cause it will **not** be a face-to-face talk.)

(B) Come up with some crazy-complex Jack-inspired plan to save the day—or at least save your sense of smell.

(C) Buy a gas mask.

(D) Peace out! Time to get a new buddy!

3. It's the monster apocalypse! How far will you go to reunite with your buddy?

(A) I will battle to the ends of this earth until we are together again!

(B) I'll try—but not, like, **extra** hard.

(C) I'll give my buddy a cool sword and then—bye! On your own!

(D) Ehh, my pal can handle anything. I'm not worried. We don't need to hang out again. Ever.

4. Do you each know a pretty awful secret about each other?

(A) And it doesn't matter? Yes!

(B) Like I'd really tell you that!

(C) What's it worth to you?

5. Got a secret handshake?

Ⓐ Yes. But neither of us can remember it.

Ⓑ Working on it!

Ⓒ No. Tried once. Decided never to do it again after the broken fingers and bloody noses.

6. You're accidentally handcuffed to your best friend? Is that an issue?

Ⓐ No. Until my best friend needs to use the toilet.

Ⓑ Maybe. Is this that friend with the bad breath?

Ⓒ Yes! Our friendship is as much about not being together as it is about being together.

7. You and your best friend pull off a heroic save-the-world mission. BUT! You're both captured and sent into eternal orbit. Who gets to ride shotgun in the spaceship?

Ⓐ We share shotgun. It's tight—but we get to ride **together**!

Ⓑ My best friend.

Ⓒ Me!

Ⓓ The weird alien hitchhiker we picked up.

8. Do you know your best bud's phone number by heart?

Ⓐ Together, my best friend and I have chosen to communicate **ONLY** via Morse code in-game chat.

Ⓑ Yes.

Ⓒ I think it has a 7 in it. . . . And maybe a 19?

Ⓓ Bananas!

9. When you grow up, what will you name after your best friend?

Ⓐ Pet.

Ⓑ Car.

Ⓒ Lucky socks.

Ⓓ Dirty socks.

10. Your best bud turns out to be a nose picker.

Ⓐ That makes two of us (darn it).

Ⓑ Will recommend professional help.

Ⓒ It's over!

SCORING

Give yourself 5 points for every (A) answer,
4 points for every (B), 3 for every (C), and 1 for every (D).

_____ (A) × 5 = _____
_____ (B) × 4 = _____
_____ (C) × 3 = _____
_____ (D) × 1 = _____

TOTAL _____

Total points:

40–50: Best friends forever. Nothing can tear you two apart!

20–39: Good friends. You're there for each other most of the time. But honestly, not Hall of Famers.

0–19: Um . . . it might be time to find a new best buddy.

Draw a map of your neighborhood—then add monsters! Or create a town or city from scratch, using just your imagination!

COSTUME CHANGE!

Throughout the series, Jack and his buddies wear a bunch of different outfits. Dream up your own radical warrior wardrobe by tracing and drawing over the characters below!

S.O.S.

Stuck in a tree house, like Jack was—
and need to send a message to someone?
Don't worry—this book can help!

STEP #1: Write your note on the back of
the next page.

STEP #2: Carefully remove the page
with a trusty pair of scissors.

STEP #3: Fold it into a paper airplane.

STEP #4: Launch that sucker!

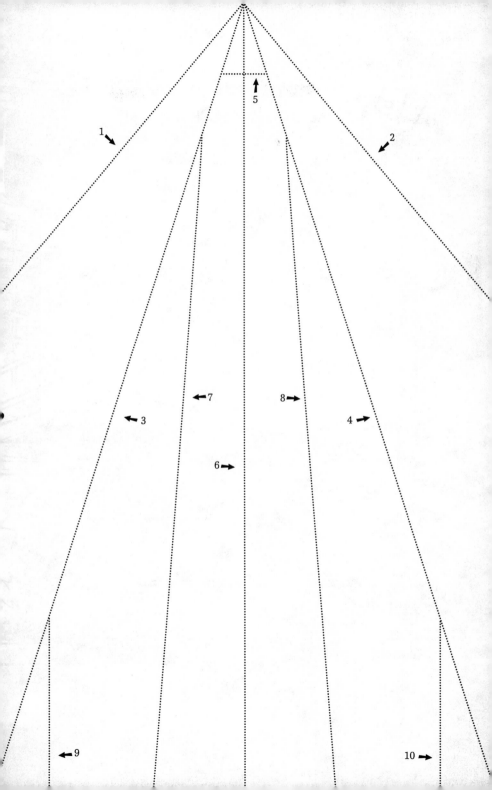

Help! WRITE YOUR PAPER
AIRPLANE NOTE HERE!

_____

_____

_____

_____

_____

_____

_____

_____

_____

_____

YOUR OWN PLAYLIST!

It's no secret that June loves music. What are your seven favorite jams? Bonus points for songs that you listen to while reading *The Last Kids on Earth*!

Today's Date:
_____

1.) _____

2.) _____

3.) _____

4.) _____

5.) _____

6.) _____

7.) _____

Write your own cool hero line here!

24

HEROIC ONE-LINERS!

Jack has said some pretty killer things to monsters. Write down some heroic stuff you would say if you were staring down a big beastie! Some of Jack's better lines . . .

"Hey! Monster face! Get a life!"
"Let's dance, monster pants!"
"No one messes with Earth on my watch!"

YOUR OWN COOL LINES!

_____

_____

_____

_____

_____

_____

_____

_____

_____

_____

 FUN FACT:

Rover is inspired by Max Brallier's childhood dog, Champ.

QUINT'S GADGETS AND GIZMOS

Salutations, friends! It is I, Quint! I hope you are enjoying your time with this whimsical tome. Please peruse my collection of gadgets. They may someday prove useful!

Glue Thrower, Goo Slower

Tactical Belt

Smoke Flash capsule.

Insta-Flame tablet.

Nintendo 3DS.

Acid Eye Blast capsule.

Stink Bomb.

Little Hug Monster-Stopping Juice Grenades

Lemon juice.

Divexol Lyzetide.

Pop Rocks.

Extra-strength dandruff shampoo.

Mayonnaise.

Honey dijon salad dressing.

June Bait

Chocolate-covered June shirt.

Not a fan of the June Bait.

Sweat-stained pits.

The Scream Machine

Retro MP3 player

Egg timer.

Quint's Maximum Decibels Attach-O tape.

Speaker. The volume goes all the way to 11!

The BOOMerang
(a weapon that goes boom)

Smoke bombs.

Sparklers.

Classic boomerang shape.

My patented Quint's Post-Apocalyptic Action Supplies, Inc. Trademark.

QUINT

 FUN FACT:

The first Last Kids on Earth book took Max Brallier nearly seven hundred days to write.

The following contraption is not for the faint of heart and should by no means be attempted at home, assuming your world has not yet been ravaged by zombie and/or monster hordes:

The Couch-a-pult

CREATE YOUR OWN QUINT GADGET!

Arrows and labels will prove useful.

Meet Rover!

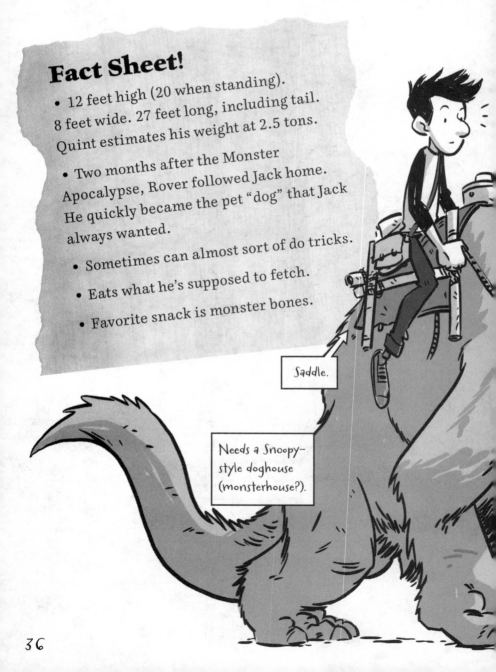

Fact Sheet!

- 12 feet high (20 when standing). 8 feet wide. 27 feet long, including tail. Quint estimates his weight at 2.5 tons.

- Two months after the Monster Apocalypse, Rover followed Jack home. He quickly became the pet "dog" that Jack always wanted.

- Sometimes can almost sort of do tricks.

- Eats what he's supposed to fetch.

- Favorite snack is monster bones.

Saddle.

Needs a Snoopy-style doghouse (monsterhouse?).

YOUR MONSTER PET

If you could have a pet monster like Rover, what sort of creature would you choose? Missile-breathing dragon? Zombified flamingo?

Design and draw it here!

OH, DEAR.

What's your pet's awesome monster name?

_____

What are your pet's cool abilities and powers?

_____

_____

_____

What sort of tricks can your pet perform?

_____

_____

_____

_____

_____

FUN FACT:

Dirk is inspired by both Wolverine and the Incredible Hulk—Max Brallier's favorite superheroes!

THE TREE HOUSE

The tree house is where Jack, June, Quint, Dirk, and Rover live! Quint and Dirk update its gadgets and defenses, while Jack and June make sure it's a fun place to hang.

Catapult #1.

Zip line (great for last-minute escapes. Also for drying socks).

Cool guy.

Mountain Dew distillery (working on perfecting the formula—currently just hot dog water and green food coloring).

Toilet bucket.

TURN THE PAGE TO MAKE
THE TREE HOUSE YOURS!

Make the Tree House YOUR House

The tree house is yours—do what you want with it! Add hammocks, Velcro walls, a special zip line—*whatever you want!*

43

Chomp, chomp, slurp...

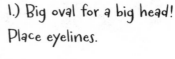

HOW TO DRAW ROVER

Get your doodle on!

1.) Big oval for a big head!
Place eyelines.

Don't forget to use a
pencil, so you can erase
mistakes!

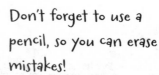

2.) Add ear and eyes.

3.) Add back of neck,
other ear, snout, and nose.

4.) Add mouth, eyebrows, and snout detail (whiskers).

5.) Now add jawline and chin.

6.) Teeth! More fur!

TOOLS OF THE TRADE

Check out of some of our heroes' *most radical* tools. They take down big bad monsters and hold back zombie hordes.

LOUISVILLE SLICER™

Electrical tape for prime monster-slaying swinging grip.

Monster teeth.

Look at that sharp tip—it's like a sword!

Dozer guts. Smells gnarly.

JUNE'S SPEAR

Carved from broom handle.

KRAK!

Razor-sharp tip.

THE GIFT THAT KEEPS ON BLASTING

Pop-out blade.

THWINK!

JACK'S MOJO

Maybe he's born with it. Maybe it's

OK, let's turn the page.

Max Brallier's favorite movie of all time is *Star Wars*.

YOUR POST-APOCALYPTIC WEAPON

It's the end of the world, monsters and zombies are everywhere, and YOU need to survive!

Is your weapon big and intimidating? Or easily hidden in case of an action-hero surprise?

It's up to you! Go wild! Add arrows and labels to point out all the coolest parts!

Now tell us about this crazy thing!

_____

_____

_____

_____

_____

_____

_____

_____

_____

_____

And don't forget to give it a rad name!

52

Ultimate End-of-the-World Armor

Jack and his buddies have armored up lots of times. Sometimes they grab stuff from around the house or school. Or sometimes it gets even more serious, like when Jack stepped inside the space marine armor from his favorite game:

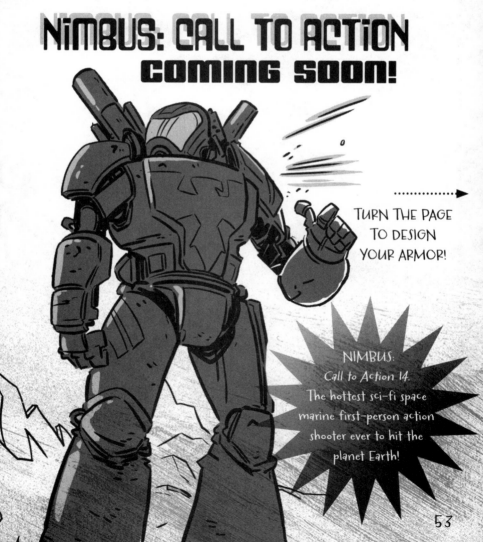

NiMBUS: CALL TO ACTION
COMING SOON!

TURN THE PAGE
TO DESIGN
YOUR ARMOR!

NIMBUS:
Call to Action 14.
The hottest sci-fi space
marine first-person action
shooter ever to hit the
planet Earth!

YOUR TURN!

Make up your own crazy armor!

Armor notes:

BIG MAMA
The Post-Apocalyptic Ride

SNOW MAMA!

TURN THE PAGE TO DESIGN YOUR VEHICLE!
·················▶

Fuzzy dice (for looking cool).

Skull hood ornament (not real, just a candle).

Horn plays the *Star Trek* theme.

Battering ram, for battering monsters.

Notches—one for each crazy giant evil monster the gang has defeated.

Plus, an ejector seat.

(Just kidding.)

(Maybe.)

57

Design Your Own End-of-the-World Vehicle!

Big Mama is rad—but you can do better! It's time to create the coolest vehicle ever, period, no limits. GO!

BOOMKART BONANZA!

BoomKarts are souped-up bumper cars designed for vehicular combat coolness. Quint added paintball blasters, defensive marble spillers, spiked tires, gas-powered slingshots, and more!

NOW IT'S YOUR TURN!

Draw your own—with gadgets, weapons, armor, and defenses. Is it built for speed or built for battling monsters? You decide!

Design your own BoomKart track!

Imagine your neighborhood or your school—then turn it into a racetrack! Add twists, turns, drops, dead ends, drawbridges, tunnels, zombies, monsters—anything goes!

HOW TO DRAW JACK

You just put your lips together and blow!

That's how to whistle, friend.

1.) Draw an oval and eyelines.

2.) Add eyes and ears.

3.) Lots of curly lines: add nose, eyebrows, and ear detail.

4.) Add Sydney Opera House sails for hair!*

5.) Define chin and add grin!

6.) Add hair shading, face details, the Slicer, and shoulders.

*EDITOR'S NOTE: Douglas Holgate is from Australia, and the Sydney Opera House is a cool reference.

Your Own Last Kids on Earth Book!

You get to be the author! What are the biggest parts of your original Last Kids adventure! Be sure to add gadgets and danger!

Who's the bad guy? _____

_____

_____

What's the scariest thing that happens? _____

_____

_____

_____

What's the funniest thing that happens? _____

_____

_____

_____

_____

Draw some Douglas Holgate-style cover art!

THE LAST KIDS ON EARTH and the

THE MONSTERS OF JOE'S PIZZA

Good-guy monsters took up residence here in Wakefield Town Square—and things haven't been the same since! They're buddies with Jack and friends, and they've battled alongside them.

Many-eyed monster.

Winged monster.

Oddly striking and dignified monster.

Steve.

Sleepy monster.

Equally sluggish.

A bunch more monsters.

JOE'S PIZZA

-Bardle-

General sort of wizardly vibe.

Funky swords for when it's time to get stabby.

Total grump face—but he's actually very sweet when you get to know him.

Who knows what strange potions lie within his magical rucksack?

Bardle is wizened, wizardly, and wise.
He's an advisor to Jack and the human heroes—
passing on knowledge about monsters, the
ultimate evil bad dude, Ṛeżžőcħ, and life in
the monster dimension. . . .

Skaelka was a vicious warrior in the monster dimension. She is scary savage and fiercely ferocious. In fact, she's kind of obsessed with chopping off bad guy heads—although Jack always seems to stop her at the last moment.

-Biggun-

Check this out: one time, Dirk and Jack turned this huge monster into a rideable beast by strapping shopping carts to his back. He became "The Biggun Mobile."

Ŗeżżŏcħ: THE BIG BAD

Ŗeżżŏcħ the Ancient, Destructor of Worlds is the ultimate ultra-villain! He comes from the time before time, when great battles were fought in the monster dimension. . . .

We have not yet seen Ṛeżżóċh here on Earth. Draw what YOU think this otherworldly evil might look like.

- WARG -

Warg isn't like the other monsters. All Jack and his pals know is that she's got a weird eyeball body and she's full of secrets. . . .

EYEBALL POWERS!

What if you controlled an army of eyeballs like
Warg? List some people you would spy on! Teachers?
Siblings? Weirdo neighbors? Parents? Other random
old people? List ten things you would do!

1.) _____

2.) _____

3.) _____

4.) _____

5.) _____

6.) _____

7.) _____

8.) _____

9.) _____

10.) _____

SPOT THE DIFFERENCE!

Check out the two pictures of Jack taking an apocalyptic morning stroll below. There are ten differences between the two—can you find all of them?

JOE'S PIZZA'S NEWEST MONSTER!

Draw and design a new good-guy monster who can hang out at Joe's Pizza!

I DEMAND A NEW MONSTER FRIEND! WITH LUCK, ONE WHO ALSO LIKES AXES!

MONSTER'S NAME: _____

Weapon: _____

Monster's special power: _____

Ten fun facts about your monster:

1.) _____

2.) _____

3.) _____

4.) _____

5.) _____

6.) _____

7.) _____

8.) _____

9.) _____

10.) _____

RAISE A GLASS TO OUR NEWEST ALLY!

Make Your Own Joe's Pizza Menu!

Your customers are monsters! Don't forget, monsters eat weird stuff like tongues, spiders (dead and alive), eyeballs, and creepy-crawly critters!

JOE'S PIZZA
Ristorante & Pizzeria
★ Monster Cuisine ★

PIZZA TOPPINGS:

STARTERS:

DRINKS & LIQUIDS:

DESSERT & GELATO:

UNDER NEW MANAGEMENT

Cooking with Bardle

FIND OUT THIS AND MORE WHEN YOU SUBSCRIBE TO MY YOUTUBE CHANNEL AND PODCAST *: MONSTER MEAL PREPERATION ON AN INTESTINE-STRING BUDGET.

* Internet no longer exists, thanks to Monster-Zombie Apocalypse.

Recipe:
BUGS ON A LOG

Raisins.

Peanut butter.

Celery.

1.) SPREAD SOME PEANUT BUTTER ON CELERY THAT YOUR PARENTS HAVE CUT FOR YOU OR THAT CAME ALREADY CUT FROM THE GROCERY STORE.

2.) PLACE RAISINS ON TOP TO TASTE. LIVE BUGS ARE ALSO ACCEPTABLE, BUT THEY MAY CRAWL AWAY IF THEY DON'T STICK TO THE PEANUT BUTTER.

3.) IF USING RAISINS, DO NOT SERVE TO BIGGUN, AS HE IS HIGHLY ALLERGIC. MONSTER SKIN ALLERGIES ARE FRIGHTENING TO BEHOLD, EVEN TO THOSE WITH THE STEELIEST CONSTITUTIONS.

 FUN FACT:

Max Brallier's second favorite movie is *Indiana Jones and the Temple of Doom.*

OTHER MONSTERS!

There are monsters in Wakefield that Jack and his buddies don't even know! Name 'em! Write about 'em! Add fun facts!

NAME: _____

FUN FACTS:

_____

_____

_____

_____

_____

_____

_____

NAME: _____

FUN FACTS:

_____

_____

_____

_____

_____

NAME: _____

FUN FACTS:

_____

_____

FUN FACTS:

_____

_____

_____

_____

 FUN FACT:

When he was a kid, Max had a tree house in his backyard.
It wasn't fancy, but it did have a zip line!

HOW TO DRAW BARDLE

QUINT. WHY DO THOSE EARTH CREATURES STARE THUSLY?

Ah. I believe they are ascertaining how best to draw you, friend Bardle.

1.) Draw circle for top of the head, place eyeline and nose guides.

2.) Add ears and eyes. Be sure to leave plenty of room for his mouth and beard!

3.) Add stern
eyebrows, nostrils,
and bumpy scalp!

4.) Add earrings,
cheekbones, and the
start of the mustache.

5.) Finish beard, add
shoulders and mighty
sword hilt!

ZOMBIFY THE HEROES!

It's time for Jack, June, Dirk, and Quint to get ZOMBIFIED! Trace over the lines and give them lots of ghoulish features—the grosser, the better!

Thrull Interrogates Author Max Brallier!

Thrull first appeared as a tough warrior and monster hunter. But in fact, he was secretly working as a servant of Ṛeżżőcħ, manipulating Jack in order to bring Ṛeżżőcħ to this world. Now he's back, and he's got some questions.

Thrull: First, why the name Thrull?

Max: I wanted to do Krull, but then I realized *I* didn't invent that name—it's from the movie *Krull*. So I made up a new name that sounded like it: THRULL!

Thrull: Second, why the name Max?

Max: Ask my parents! All I know is, when I was a kid, I never met anyone else named Max. The only Maxes were dogs. Everyone was like, "Oh, I have a dog named Max, it's a great name for a dog, yadda yadda yadda." I was like, yeah, cool, whatever, but I'm a human, and I think it's a fine name for a human.

Thrull: Are you Jack?

Max: No, I'm Max. But am I like Jack? Sorta. . . . Jack's like the cool, brave, funny version of me. I'm like the dorky, geeky version of Jack—which is saying a lot, because Jack is already super dorky and super geeky.

Thrull: Why did you make me so monstrous and evil? Not sure how I feel about that.

Max: Someone's gotta be the bad dude. Just happens that I made that someone you.

Thrull: Why couldn't you make me clever, like Quint?

Max: You *are* clever! You had that whole clever plan with the bestiary! I mean, I think and hope it was clever—I wrote it, and it seemed like a clever bad-guy plan to me!

Thrull: What scares you?

Max: Lots of stuff. Rats, mice, snakes, heights, the deep deep ocean, deep deep space—also missing deadlines and bad reviews of my books.

Thrull: How come I can never put Jack in his place like June does?

Max: June's tougher and cooler than you. Sorry—it's just a fact, dude.

Thrull: Where do you write my tales of adventure? Office, poolside, cabin, tree house?

Max: First of all, they aren't *your* tales of adventure—

you're the bad guy! But to answer the actual question, I do most of my writing in coffee shops in New York City and in restaurants on the road.

Thrull: How do you write? Pen, typewriter, computer?

Max: I use a blue pen and a notebook to jot down ideas, because I get ideas everywhere. I even had the idea for you in the shower—true story! When it's time to write the real book, I use a computer.

Thrull: Do you describe the characters to Douglas Holgate? Tell him what they look like? Or does he read the book and then come up with how they look? What did you tell him about me? I'm really better looking than this, you know.

Max: A bit of both. Basically, I write a few dinky words, then Doug takes those few dinky words and turns them into something pure awesome. And you he made pure evil.

Thrull: Do you know right now what's going to happen in, like, books six, seven, twenty?

Max: Yes and no. I've got a plan for the grand finale, and I've got a few ideas for what happens along the way. Each book will continue to feel bigger and more epic. And I want to see the heroes fail a bunch of times—I don't want them to just win, win, win.

Thrull: What's it like to be a human? If living isn't all about destroying Earth, what do you do all day? I don't get that.

Max: I play Ping-Pong, ride my bike, play video games, read books, sit on my butt, take photos, daydream, and hang with my family.

Thrull: How do the books end? Do the heroes survive? Find happiness? Do I?

Max: You'll have to wait and see! I'll tell you this much, though: I hate when endings are totally perfect and happy. I like a little bit of sadness and loss—even in a happy ending.

Thrull: Why did you make my personality so, well, wooden? And don't cop out and blame it on your editor.

Max: Oh, I get it—it's a joke, because of the tree thing*? Ha. Ha. Very funny.

Thrull: Why did you ever think loud music would distract me from my evil plot? What is wrong with you?

Max: It worked, didn't it?

Thrull: Will Jack and June ever kiss?

Max: Dude! None of your business! I'm out—this interview is *over!*

*

A VILLAINOUS NEW SPECIES!

Dozers, Vine-Thingies, and Winged Wretches are, like, their own categories of monster. Create your own species!

SPECIES NAME: _____

MAIN ATTACK: _____

_____

BIGGEST WEAKNESS: _____

_____

_____

WEIRD FACTS: _____

_____

_____

_____

_____

_____

_____

YOUR VERY OWN COSMIC SERVANT

Ŗeżżŏ̌ch's Cosmic Servants are the BIGGEST and BADDEST monsters—like Blarg, Thrull, and the King Wretch. Design your own here!

What is the Cosmic Servant's name? _____

_____

What are its evil powers? _____

_____

What is the scariest thing about this monster? _____

_____

_____

What is the grossest thing about this monster? _____

_____

_____

_____

What would you do if YOU encountered this creature?

_____

_____

_____

_____

Zombify a Buddy!

Draw friends or family members or even pets— but zombify them! To get extra weird, tape a photo of them here and draw all over them!

MMUHHH...

MONSTER LANGUAGE DECODED!

Quint got his hands on Bardle's private notebook, and it turns out he writes in a completely different monster language!

Use the code below to write secret messages to your buddies in Bardle speak! Make photocopies of the code for your friends so you can trade messages.

A – ⋕
B – ▲
C – ⚯
D – ♌
E – ❮
F – ♀
G – ⊼
H – ◗

I – □
J – ✳
K – ☉
L – ◠
M – ➴
N – ⊕
O – ⊥
P – ▼
Q – ◠

R – ■
S – ⊖
T – ⋀
U – ☿
V – ▽
W – ◐
X – ⊐
Y – ≡
Z – ⊠

Bwa-ha-ha! Villainous laughter!

HOW TO DRAW EVIE

She's a fiend! Let's learn how to draw her anyway!

1.) Draw oval and eyelines.

Be sure to leave room for her hair— it's pretty big!

2.) Add eyes and curved nose.

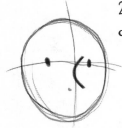

3.) Add eyebrows and ears.

4.) Define chin.
Add evil grin and
ear detail.

5.) Add wild hair!
Make sure you
add extra curls!

6.) Draw her
cape, glasses,
and earrings.
Here's lookin'
at you, kid!

 FUN FACT: Max Brallier sometimes writes under a different name: Jack Chabert.

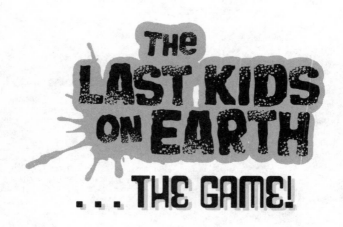

THE LAST KIDS ON EARTH

... THE GAME!

Jack and Quint love video games. Their favorite is the space marine shooter *Nimbus: Call to Action*.

Imagine you could create your own video game about the Last Kids on Earth!

What's the title? _____

_____

What type of game is it? _____

_____

_____

Who's the big final boss at the end of the game? ____

_____

_____

What vehicles do the characters use? _____

_____

What's the best part of the game? _____

_____

_____

_____

_____

_____

TURN THE PAGE TO DESIGN
YOUR GAME'S COVER! ··········▶

A good video game needs a good cover. Draw some awesome art for your Last Kids on Earth game!

Jack made his very own License to Kill Monsters card—and it was kind of lame.

But here is an actually awesome license that you can cut out and carry with you!

✂ cut here!

The Last Kids on Earth theme song!

Our heroes have a rad tree house, a mighty pet, and a crazy vehicle. But they don't have a theme song . . . yet.

Write some killer lyrics and give the gang the awesome theme song they deserve.

You know I love music, so make this song extra-dope!

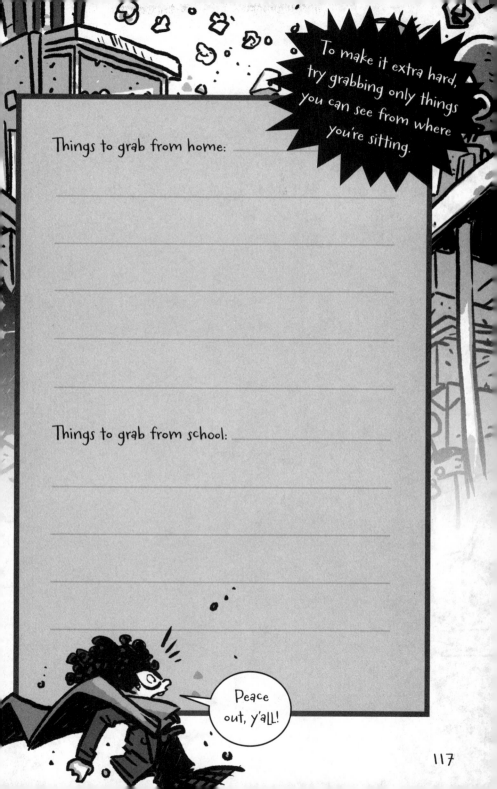

Things to grab from home: _____

_____

_____

_____

_____

_____

Things to grab from school: _____

_____

_____

_____

_____

To make it extra hard, try grabbing only things you can see from where you're sitting.

Peace out, y'all!

Your Monster-Zombie Apocalypse Plan!

If monsters and zombies come—what's
your plan? Will you retreat to a hangout
like Jack in the tree house? Or will you hop
into a vehicle like Big Mama and get out of
town? Write down your plans!

A Last Kids on Earth comic?
THAT'S WHAT'S UP!

Write and draw your own comic starring Jack, June, Quint, Dirk, and Rover!

Soon . . .

Suddenly . . .

And then:

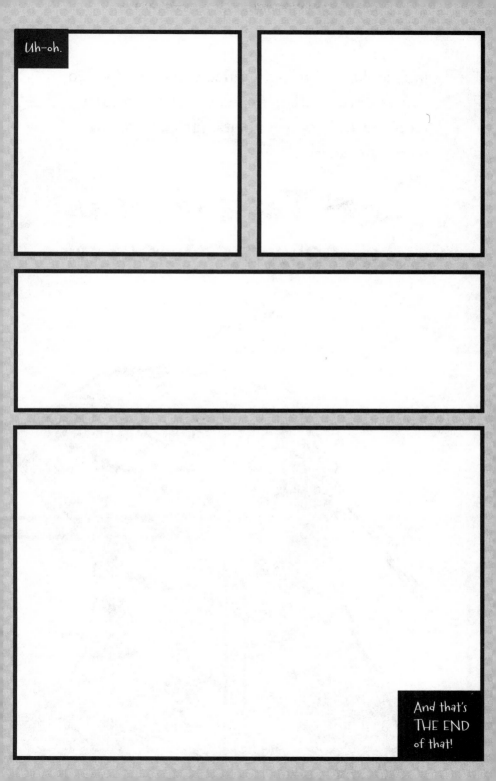

Jack looks at life like a video game—and video games have challenges you complete to earn trophies and achievements. Jack created his own. They are . . .

Feats of Apocalyptic Success!

FEAT: Mad Hatter!

Steal the hats off five zombies.

FEAT: Outrun!

Beat a zombie in a footrace.

FEAT: Say Cheese!

Take a photo with someone you knew before they got zombified.

FEAT: House Hunter

Explore 50 different abandoned houses.

FEAT: Get an Awesome Pet

Rover. 'Nuff said!

Your OWN Feats of Apocalyptic Success!

What if you were alone in a world of zombies, monsters, and buddies? What Feats of Apocalyptic Success would you create? Title them, describe them, and draw some worthy badges!

FEAT: _____

_____

FEAT: _____

_____

FEAT: _____

_____

Feats of Everyday Success!

Your real life may not be as action-packed as Jack's—but you can still create rad feats! Create everyday life challenges that you're going to complete!

FEAT: _____

_____

FEAT: _____

_____

FEAT: _____

_____

FEAT: _____
_____

FEAT: _____
_____

FEAT: _____
_____

List-A-Rama!

Jack tries to help the monsters understand Earth. It's time to list the things that YOU would recommend to someone new to this dimension.

List 10 movies a new friend must watch:

1.) _____

2.) _____

3.) _____

4.) _____

5.) _____

6.) _____

7.) _____

8.) _____

9.) _____

10.) _____

 FUN FACT:

Just like our heroes, Max went to Parker Middle School. But there were no zombies.

10 books a new friend must read:

1.) _____

2.) _____

3.) _____

4.) _____

5.) _____

6.) _____

7.) _____

8.) _____

9.) _____

10.) _____

Egads, this tome is riveting!

10 games or activities a
new friend must try:

1.)

2.)

3.)

4.)

5.)

6.)

7.)

8.)

9.)

10.)

MONSTER-ZOMBIE PICNIC!

When the gang had a picnic to scope out monster territory, they brought Quint's vintage lunch box, loaded with Reese's Pieces.

What would YOU pack for the perfect post-apocalyptic picnic hangout with your buddies?

LIST OR DRAW YOUR MONSTER-ZOMBIE PICNIC SNACKS!

_____

_____

_____

_____

_____

_____

_____

_____

_____

_____

 FUN FACT:

Max owns more than one hundred vintage Star Wars toys and action figures. Yep, he's _super_ cool.

WHAT'S YOUR POST-APOCALYPTIC MONSTER NAME?

First letter of your FIRST NAME

A – grub

B – beetle

C – terrible

D – bunion

E – stale

F – whiskery

G – stingy

H – X-ray

I – bitter

J – spotted

K – knuckle

L – sour

M –claw

N – gooey

O – voracious

P – repugnant

Q – toenail

R – elbow

S – tentacle

T – captain

U – hairy

V – stormy

W – crusty

X – wicked

Y – wartomous

Z – onion

First letter of your
LAST NAME

A – menace	N – quicksand
B – slime	O – demon
C – boil	P – earwax
D – grimace	Q – vine
E – puke bug	R – wormongulous
F – snail	S – sludge
G – vomit	T – poison
H – brains	U – eyeball
I – breath	V – king
J – crusher	W – savage
K – mud	X – sawtooth
L – roach	Y – explosion
M – eggs	Z – sparkle

HELLO
my monster name is

CREATE YOUR OWN HOLIDAY!

Jack and his pals created their very own post-apocalyptic Christmas. They started new traditions, like a dance showdown, a wrapping paper sword duel, and a king of the hill battle. Now it's your turn to create your own holiday!

What's it called? _____

What's being celebrated? _____

_____

How often do you celebrate? _____

_____

_____

What's the BEST part of your holiday?

_____

_____

Are there awesome parts of other holidays that you'll throw into your totally original holiday?

_____

_____

_____

Are there gifts? Or fireworks? OR BOTH?! _____

_____

_____

What are the traditions? _____

_____

_____

_____

_____

THE BESTIARY

Jack and his buddies catalog and research the many monsters that have taken up residence in Wakefield. Turn the page to see what they've learned. . . .

CLASSIC ZOMBIE
(Undeadius Reanimatedus)

Constant, creepy moaning.

Those empty eyes—they're spooksville.

MMUHHH...

Bite you and you're one of them. Undead!

Stink like hot garbage.

Slow, until they get close—then fast!

ZOMBIE BALL
(Undeadius Rollaroundus)

Total nightmare fuel.

Zombie faces, just being horrible and terrifying.

Hall pass.

Zombie hands, pulling it forward.

Quint Notes: A lurching mass of the undead; possibly created by one zombie tripping down the stairs and taking every zombie with him, snowball style.

Known Habitats: School, near the teacher's lounge.

Principal Attack: Rolling aimlessly, like a bitey tumbleweed.

Strengths: Flattening momentum.

Weaknesses: Doors, small hallways, turnstiles.

HAIRY EYEBALL MONSTER
(Pilosus Acutus Oculus)

Pupil opens to allow monster verbal communication (roars, shrieks, howls).

Iris color changes depending on mood, weather.

One single, massive eyeball.

When angered, hair stands on end, forming razor-sharp quills.

Quint Notes: Ability to launch its quills at an enemy with crossbow force, distance, and accuracy.

Known Habitats: Old South Graveyard.

Principal Attack: Needle onslaught.

Strengths: Rolling ability makes for easy, unobstructed travel and pursuit. Undefeated at staring contests.

Weaknesses: Bright flashes, moderate ragweed allergy, contact lenses.

LITTLE GUYS
(Tinius Furrius)

No eyes, hunt by smell locators located within saliva ducts.

Travel in packs.

PUKE BUG KING
(Rex Putidus Insectus)

Revenge on its mind—angry about all those ants you've stepped on!

Wings? Let's hope not.

Body formed from hundreds of thousands of monster insects joining together. Teamwork!

Emits a deafening series of clicking, clacking, and hissing noises.

Releases a sweet, overpowering stench.

Facial features evident.

Quint Notes: A slew of tiny, monstrous insects, formed together to create a "King Bug." P.B.K.'s brain is as yet unknown.

Known Habitats: June's neighbors' house (the Gradwohls).

Principal Attack: Crushing YOU like a bug, for once.

Strengths: Unbreakable shell—is anything stronger than a gulbillion exoskeletons acting as one?!

Weaknesses: Citronella-and-bug-spray flamethrower.

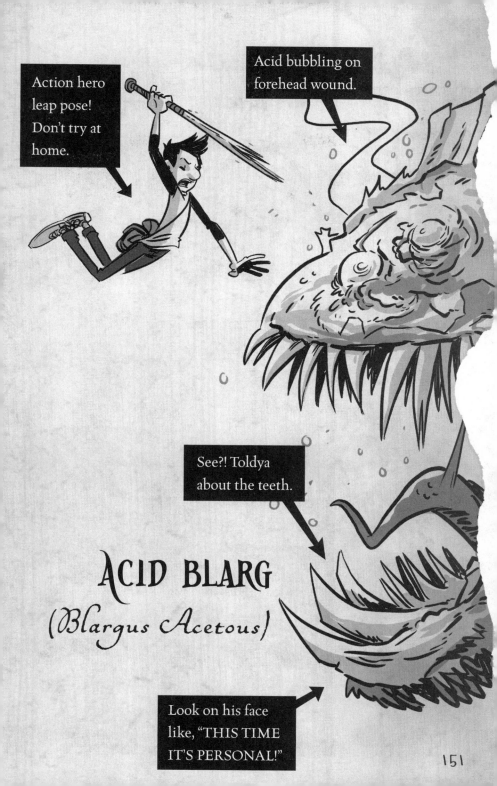

DOZER *(Bula Ploeg)*

Will eat zombies, but seems to prefer the living.

Tiny brain. Not much upstairs.

Travels alone, unlike the zombies.

Dead zombie. Oxymoron?

Look at the muscles! This dude lifts.

Quint Notes: A towering, territorial mound of monster muscle. Will stop at nothing when it has eyes on next meal.

Known Habitats: All over Wakefield.

Principal Attack: Bum rushing at high speed. Like a bull—but an evil monster version.

Strengths: Crushing bones. Blind fury.

Weaknesses: Dumb as a box of teeth.

153

THRULL
(Tradere Vilis)

Radical hammer-club-mallet dealie.

Generally humanoid face.

Cologne stench.

Absolutely CRUSHING No-Shave November.

Compasses, gizmos, and beastly thingamabobs.

Fang necklace. So you know he's mean.

Opposable thumbs.

Bone and skull jewelry (probably not a good sign ...).

154

Horrific eyeholes clawed from bark.

Evil stench emanating!

Still rocking the radical beard!

Vine-Thingies covering his body .

Woody tree-trunk legs.

THRULL THE TREE BEAST
(Vilis Deku Woodenus)

155

THE KING WRETCH
(Wretchedus Rex)

Quint Notes: The alpha Wretch; much bigger than an average Wretch and much stronger. Best described as "nightmare fuel."

Known Habitats: High above Wakefield; Comically Speaking.

Principal Attack: Hypnosis, followed by talon-grab 'n' smash.

Strengths: Telepathy, flight, breakneck speed, general terror-inducing.

Weaknesses: The Scrapken.

Battle scars.

Bone wings.

WORMUNGULOUS
(Graboidous)

Poor vision.

Approximately 1,000 knife-like denticles.

Quint Notes: Part millipede, part centipede, part earthworm, part freight train.

Known Habitats: The Circle One Mall

Principal Attack: Bursting out of the ground, jaws-first; earthquake flop.

Strengths: Stealth mode, skin like a tank.

Weaknesses: Poor eyesight. Bad at hiding.

Jaws like a rusty lawnmower.

Kinda squishy here! Might want tickles?

Cosmically bad intentions!

Strange, snapping, twitching tail.

Action figure bits.

GHAZT (Mighty Gnawus)

THE SCRAPKEN
(Junkcelcior Maximus)

"Just woke up" face.

One eye—which is one too many.

Quint Notes: Possesses many qualities of a kraken, but instead of water, it lives in trash.

Known Habitats: Big Al's Junkyard; perhaps elsewhere?

Principal Attack: Ripping enemies limb from limb.

Strengths: Multiple, tentacled limbs, the size of a city bus.

Weaknesses: He's a trash guy.

UGLY MONSTER
(Only a Facex a Mother Could Lovus)

Gills for breathing, hearing, and sensing.

No eyes. Which just makes it freakier. . . .

Mouth cannot close—constantly drooling.

EWW, NAKED MONSTER!

Elbow blades.

Arm? Foot? Both?

OIL MONSTER
(Fossilfuelus Prodigium)

This eye's near-sighted.

This eye's far-sighted.

This eye's juuuust right.

Zero traction.

Uh-oh—looks like Jack and his friends skipped a few pages! It's up to *you* to complete the bestiary. Design three new monsters!

NAME:

Notes:

_____

_____

_____

Known Habitats:

_____

Principal Attack:

_____

Strengths:

_____

Weaknesses:

_____

NAME:

Notes:

_____

_____

_____

Known Habitats:

_____

Principal Attack:

_____

Strengths:

_____

Weaknesses:

_____

172

NAME:

Notes:

_____

_____

_____

Known Habitats:

_____

Principal Attack:

_____

Strengths:

_____

Weaknesses:

_____

Time Travel!

It's time capsule time! Write a message to yourself: fill it with secret thoughts, a list of your favorite things, and your hopes and dreams for the next year!

Then fold over the page and tape it shut.

See how it says "DO NOT OPEN FOR ONE YEAR"? Do that.

Until next year!

Do you remember what you were thinking a year ago? Probably not! But this time next year, YOU WILL!

TURN THE PAGE
TO WRITE YOUR
NOTES ·············➤

DO NOT OPEN
FOR ONE YEAR!

fold here

TIME CAPSULE MESSAGE to Your Future Self: _____

_____

_____

Favorite things right now: _____

_____

_____

Things you hate right now: _____

_____

_____

Hopes and dreams for next year: _____

_____

_____

_____

Your turn!

YOUR OWN
Last Kids on Earth Book!

Now it's your turn. Write your own original story about Jack, June, Quint, and Dirk. Or write about the bad guys! Or write about Rover!

Feeling stuck? Here are a few ideas. . . .

Figure out how the heroes will escape a horde of zombies, working together, combining their unique strengths to succeed. Or . . .

June and a friendly monster imagine their own amusement park. One that both monsters and humans can enjoy.

Create a new Feat of Apocalyptic Success and send
the characters after it! _____

_____

_____

_____

_____

_____

_____

_____

The drama, it's ... so high-octane. . . .

Yeah. It's all like a larger metaphor for life, really.

Simile.

Write all about what Evie and Thrull would do if they hung out together for a day! _____

_____

_____

_____

_____

_____

_____

_____

_____

_____

_____

 FUN FACT: Max has a sister who is eight years younger than him. She's rad.

Now just write whatever you want! _____

_____

_____

_____

_____

_____

_____

_____

_____

_____

_____

 FUN FACT:

Max Brallier's favorite book of all time is *Bart Simpson's Guide to Life*.

MAX BRALLIER!

(maxbrallier.com) is the *New York Times* bestselling author of more than thirty books and games, including the Last Kids on Earth series. He writes both children's books and adult books, including the Galactic Hot Dogs series and the pick-your-own-path adventure *Can YOU Survive the Zombie Apocalypse?* He has written books for properties including *Adventure Time, Regular Show, Steven Universe, Uncle Grandpa,* and *Poptropica.*

Under the pen name Jack Chabert, he is the creator and author of the Eerie Elementary series for Scholastic Books as well as the author of the *New York Times* bestselling graphic novel *Poptropica: Book 1: Mystery of the Map.* Previously, he worked in the marketing department at St. Martin's Press. Max lives in New York with his wife, Alyse, who is way too good for him. His daughter, Lila, is simply the best.

Follow Max on Twitter @MaxBrallier.

The author building his own tree house as a kiddo.

DOUGLAS HOLGATE!

(skullduggery.com.au) has been a freelance comic book artist and illustrator based in Melbourne, Australia, for more than ten years. He's illustrated books for publishers such as HarperCollins, Penguin Random House, Hachette, and Simon & Schuster, including the Planet Tad series, Cheesie Mack, Case File 13, and *Zoo Sleepover*.

Douglas has illustrated comics for Image, Dynamite, Abrams, and Penguin Random House. He's currently working on the self-published series Maralinga, which received grant funding from the Australian Society of Authors and the Victorian Council for the Arts, as well as the all-ages graphic novel *Clem Hetherington and the Ironwood Race*, published by Scholastic Graphix, both co-created with writer Jen Breach.

Follow Douglas on Twitter @douglasbot.

THE MONSTER-BATTLING FUN DOESN'T STOP HERE!

Check out more books in the bestselling

THE LAST KIDS ON EARTH SERIES.

Stay tuned for *The Last Kids on Earth and the Midnight Blade*, available Fall 2019!